P9-DBH-920

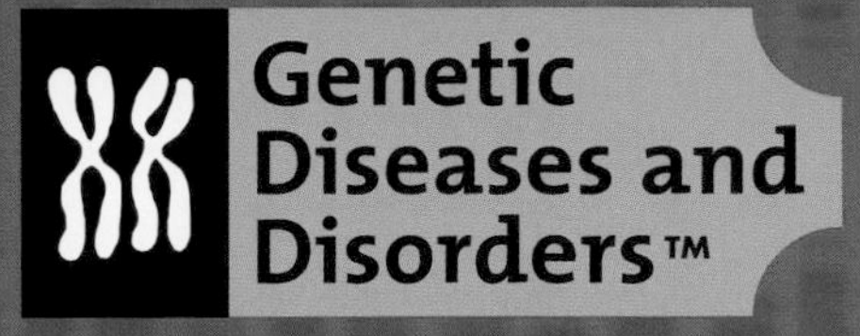


# Down Syndrome

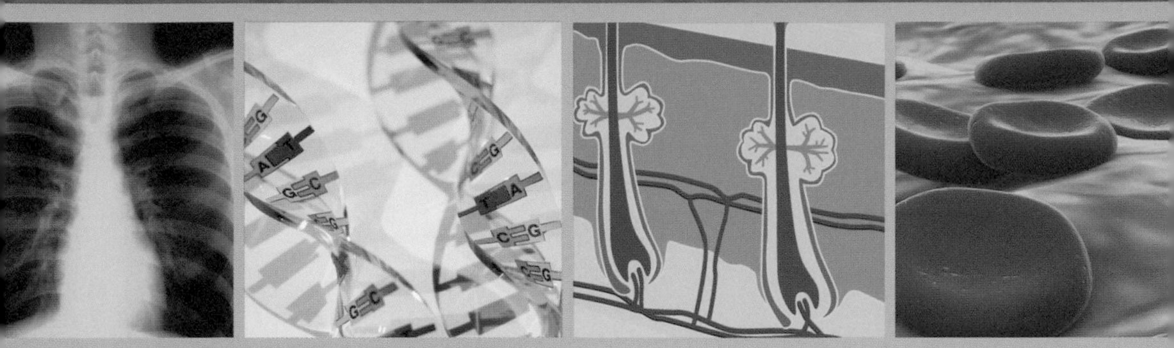

Phillip Margulies

The Rosen Publishing Group, Inc., New York

Published in 2007 by The Rosen Publishing Group, Inc.
29 East 21st Street, New York, NY 10010



First Edition



**Library of Congress Cataloging-in-Publication Data**

Margulies, Phillip.
Down syndrome / Phillip Margulies.—1st ed.
p. cm.—(Genetic diseases and disorders)
Includes bibliographical references and index.
ISBN 1-4042-0695-7 (library binding)
1. Down syndrome—Juvenile literature.
I. Title. II. Series.
RC571.M37 2007
616.85'8842—dc22

2005028916

*Manufactured in the United States of America*

**On the cover:** Background: Detail of a human karyotype showing trisomy-21; Foreground: Model of DNA double helix.

# Contents

# Introduction

You have probably seen a child or grown-up with Down syndrome, a genetic disorder that affects physical and mental development. Because it shows up in outward features like the shape of the face and the head, people with Down syndrome are easy to recognize. Teenagers and adults with Down syndrome tend to be short and heavy, with the backs of their heads somewhat flattened. In addition, they have a similar assortment of health problems. For example, nearly half of the people born with Down syndrome suffer from serious heart defects. The British physician John Langdon Down (1828–1896), who described the syndrome in 1866, wrote that "when placed side by side," people with Down syndrome look like "members of the same family." To a degree, this is true. But, of course, people with Down syndrome also resemble members of their own families.

There are mental and emotional similarities among people with Down syndrome as well. Although some people with the disorder

A young woman with Down syndrome walks with her father. People with Down syndrome tend to be sociable and friendly. Like most people, they generally form their strongest loving bonds with family members.

have intelligence within the normal range, most have some intellectual disabilities. Both children and adults with Down syndrome tend to be happy, gentle, friendly, and affectionate.

We now know that Down syndrome is caused by an error in the copying of genetic material when it is passed from parents to their offspring. The thousands of genes that encode the human body's instructions for physical and mental development are contained in forty-six chromosomes. These chromosomes are found in the nucleus of every cell in our bodies. As a result of a genetic error, people with Down syndrome have an extra copy of one of these chromosomes in many or all of their body cells. To learn more about this disorder, scientists have had to unlock some of the deepest mysteries of life.

# The History of Down Syndrome Research

# 1

Since Down syndrome arises from a common error in a basic life process, it is safe to assume that Down syndrome has existed for as long as there have been human beings. Medical historians have identified cases of Down syndrome in children depicted in European paintings made as early as the fifteenth century.

Nevertheless, for most of human history, nobody singled out the condition and gave it a name. In premodern times, people with Down syndrome were probably lumped together with other people with intellectual disabilities and those suffering many different kinds of mental illnesses. However, this changed as our knowledge of human beings developed. By the 1800s, European physicians were making more careful

People with mental disorders have suffered misunderstanding and poor treatment for most of human history. This engraving by the English artist William Hogarth (1697–1764) highlights the difficult environment in a ward for mental patients at Bethlehem Hospital in London.

observations. Eventually, people with mental illnesses (like mania or depression) were classified differently from people with intellectual disabilities (like mental retardation). The stage was set for the discovery of Down syndrome as a separate disorder.

## Describing the Disorder

Correctly identifying a disorder is a crucial step in finding its causes and its treatment. John Langdon Down, who described the disorder that bears his name, deserves credit for making that crucial first step.

John Langdon Down (shown here in an 1866 photograph) expressed surprise that no one before him had fully described the syndrome that came to bear his name. In fact, the symptoms of Down syndrome were described somewhat less completely in 1838, by Jean Etienne Dominique Esquirol (1772–1840), and in 1844, by Edouard Séguin (1812–1880).

The son of a shop owner in Cornwall, England, John Langdon Down had a scientific mind and worked with the physicist and chemist Michael Faraday (1791–1867) before deciding on a career in medicine. In 1859, he was appointed medical superintendent of the Earlwood Asylum for Idiots in Surrey. (In the 1800s, the term "idiot" was still used as a serious medical label for people with severe intellectual disabilities.) Down made many observations about the patients in his care. In 1866, he published a scientific paper in which he identified a set of patients at the hospital who bore similar physical and mental characteristics—the indicators of what we now call Down syndrome. Down did not name the condition he identified Down syndrome. Instead, he called the condition mongolism because he had a theory that these patients were throwbacks to the Mongols, common ancestors of many Europeans and Asians. Physicians used the misleading words "mongolism" and "mongoloid" for around 100 years after Down published his paper. Only in the early 1960s did the condition become widely known as "Down syndrome."

## Many Theories

During the late nineteenth and early twentieth centuries, medical scientists continued to describe children and adults with Down syndrome. They learned a great deal about people with Down syndrome and their special medical problems but relatively little about the cause of the disorder. Since evidence was scarce, there were many theories.

Most medical authorities realized fairly quickly that the resemblances between the so-called mongoloids and Asian people were very superficial. Patients with Down syndrome were found among people of Asian and African descent as well as among Europeans. Physicians noticed that older women were more likely to have a child with Down syndrome. Perhaps, some speculated, this was due to older mothers' exhaustion after a long series of pregnancies. (Babies with Down syndrome were often the last born to large families.) Now we know that an older mother is more likely to have a baby with Down syndrome regardless of whether she has previously given birth.

Other physicians noted that some members of the families of children with Down syndrome suffered from tuberculosis. They thought that tuberculosis in the mother might be a cause. Conditions such as alcoholism and thyroid deficiencies in parents can cause intellectual disabilities in children. So these, too, were suspected as causes of Down syndrome. Some scientists suspected that mental or emotional stress during pregnancy might be a factor. Other scientists suspected that catching a virus during pregnancy—which can cause other birth defects—might cause Down syndrome.

## DOWN SYNDROME AND MONGOLISM

John Langdon Down put forward his ideas in a scientific paper entitled "Observations on an Ethnic Classification of Idiots." At the time, "Mongol" and "Mongoloid" were words that Europeans used to designate the peoples of Asia. The slanting eyes and relatively flat faces of the patients Down examined suggested to him a likeness between them and what he called in his paper the "great Mongol race."

In the 1860s, physicians and biologists were excited about Charles Darwin's (1809–1882) theory of evolution. Darwin presented convincing evidence that all living things, including human beings, had evolved from earlier forms of life on Earth.

*A Mongolian woman is pictured here in traditional dress. The physical features of some Down syndrome patients led John Langdon Down to call the syndrome "mongolism." However, not all people with Down syndrome look Asian, and Down syndrome tends to occur equally in all populations around the world.*

A popular scientific theory linked to Darwin's ideas was that people suffering from some disorders were "throwbacks" to earlier stages in human development. In his paper, Down suggested that what he called mongolism was an example of a backward evolution, or retrogression, probably to some common ancestor of present-day Asians and Europeans. We know now that this is not true.

Although it was wrong, Down's theory did contain a hint of the real cause of the disorder. Down recognized that his patients suffered from problems related to heredity, the biological process by which physical and mental characteristics are passed on from one generation to the next. In other words, in a time before the discovery of genes or chromosomes, Down was correct in guessing that the syndrome was what we now call a genetic disease.

## The Genetic Connection

Gradually, more attention became focused on the likelihood that the disorder was genetic, related to biological inheritance. There was some evidence that a family in which there was one child with Down syndrome was more likely to have another child with the same condition. In other words, scientists noticed that the disorder ran in families.

Then, as more cases were found, scientists began to notice that in monozygotic twins (so-called identical twins born from the splitting of one fertilized egg), both or neither had Down syndrome. However, among dizygotic twins (fraternal twins, from two fertilized eggs), in only a few cases did both twins have the disorder. The same thing that made twins identical—their genetic inheritance—gave them both Down syndrome.

This evidence further suggested that the disease was genetic and not caused by an event like the mother catching a virus during her pregnancy.

By the 1930s, scientists knew that the blueprint for the human body was contained in packets of information found in the nucleus of every cell of the body. They called the information genes, though at that point the chemical nature of genes was unknown. They knew that the genes were bundled in structures called chromosomes, which were observable under microscopes.

## Chromosomes

In the early twentieth century, scientists did extensive research on the fruit fly, a creature convenient for genetic research because it reproduces every day and has large and relatively simple chromosomes. Through these studies, a great deal was learned about how chromosomes are involved in reproduction. Scientists knew that chromosomes came in pairs and that during reproduction each parent contributed half of his or her chromosomes to the child. They knew that normal human beings had around forty-six chromosomes. (Some thought the number was forty-eight, as lab techniques were not yet good enough for a precise count.) They also knew that errors at the chromosome level sometimes occurred during reproduction. Usually the offspring whose genetic material carried such errors did not survive, but sometimes they did. Scientists began to think that some illnesses might result from such errors.

In 1932, a Dutch ophthalmologist and medical geneticist named Petrus Johannes Waardenburg (1886–1979) came up with the correct theory of the cause of Down syndrome. He suggested that the disorder was caused by a chromosome

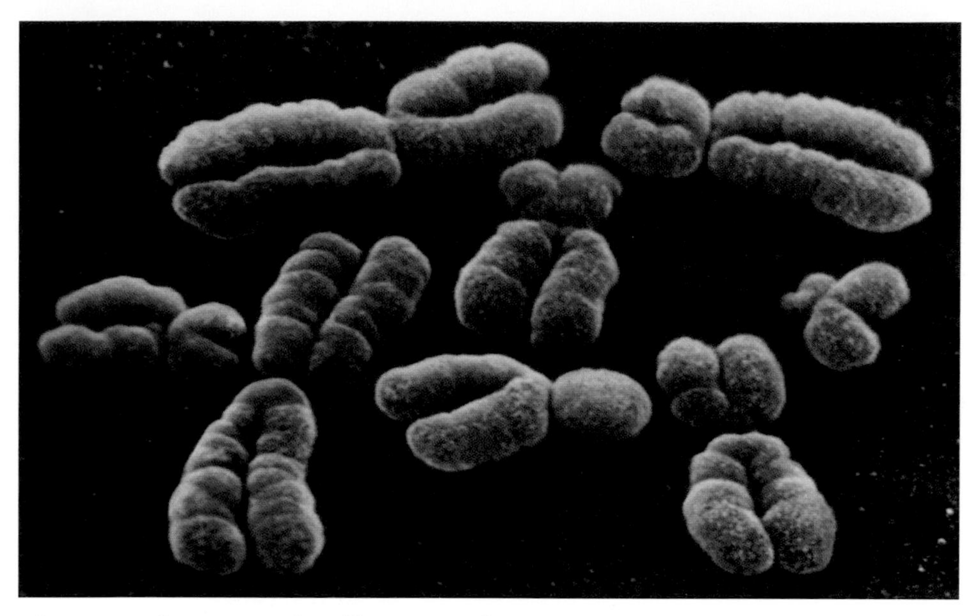

This is a photograph of human chromosomes taken with the help of an electron microscope. Each cell of the human body ordinarily contains forty-six chromosomes, arranged, as shown here, in pairs. The cells of people with Down syndrome contain forty-seven chromosomes.

abnormality called nondisjunction. Disjunction is the name scientists gave to the normal splitting of the chromosome pairs, the function that enables each parent to give half of his or her chromosomes to the child. In nondisjunction, one pair of chromosomes fails to split correctly, so the child ends up with either an extra chromosome or one too few. Waardenburg was right, but the tools of chromosome research were not yet advanced enough to confirm his theory.

# The Genetic Basis of Down Syndrome

# 2

Down syndrome is a genetic disorder, and to understand it, we have had to solve the mystery of biological inheritance. It is an understanding that has come slowly over the past 150 years.

## Uncovering the Secrets of Genetics

For all of human history, people have noticed that children tend to resemble their parents. A child might get his or her mother's eyes or his or her father's nose. Often, a little more puzzlingly, a child seems to have a feature that is absent in his or her parents but present in a grandparent. In other words, we inherit our physical traits, and maybe some of our mental traits, from previous generations.

An important first step toward understanding this process occurred in 1866. This, coincidentally, was the same year Down published his paper describing the syndrome that now bears his name. That year, an Austrian monk named Gregor Mendel (1822–1884) published a scientific paper laying out the basic laws of genetics. Mendel discovered these laws through a series of experiments with pea plants. He combined different varieties of pea plants that had distinct, easy-to-identify traits, such as height, shape, color, flower shape, and seed shape.

Mendel noticed that when he combined tall and short pea plants, he did not get medium-height offspring. Rather, the next generation included a certain percentage of tall plants and a certain percentage of short plants. When he combined light and dark pea plants, he didn't get plants with an in-between color. He got a certain percentage of light plants and a certain percentage of dark ones. When he combined plants that produced wrinkled seeds and plants that had smooth seeds, the result was the same—some wrinkled, some smooth, but none in between.

He also noted that sometimes the offspring of two short plants might be tall. But this was the case only if the short pea plants had tall ancestors. It seemed that pea plants, like human beings, could inherit a trait not present in their parents but present in the generations that preceded them.

## Identifying Genes

Mendel concluded that hidden "heredity factors" were at work. These heredity factors determined whether the offspring would have the outward trait of the mother or

Austrian monk Gregor Mendel discovered the laws of genetics and described them in a scientific paper in 1866. In his initial research, Mendel cultivated about 30,000 pea plants. It took him more than seven years to complete his research.

the father. The trait could even remain hidden for a generation or two and then suddenly reappear. Mendel didn't know what the heredity factors looked like or how they worked, but he deduced that they existed based on his observations of the outward appearance of several generations of pea plants.

Today, we call these heredity factors genes. Genes, Mendel theorized, were what carried the information that made children resemble their parents. He proposed that genes did not change. The genes passed on to the child were exact copies of the ones the parents had inherited from *their* parents. And for each trait, there were two genes, one from each parent.

Mendel had an answer for the question of why the combination of short and tall pea plants might produce a brood with some short offspring, some tall, but none of medium height. Genes, Mendel thought, were either "dominant" or "recessive." A dominant gene was always expressed over a recessive one. So a trait produced by a dominant gene always appeared in an offspring that had received a copy of that dominant gene. A child might inherit a recessive gene, and might even pass it on to the next generation, but this wouldn't make a difference in the child's appearance. The only reason we know that recessive genes exist is that sometimes a child inherits two of them. When there are two recessive genes for the same trait, the recessive genes *are* expressed. Recessive genes explain why traits sometimes skip a generation.

Scientists have learned a lot in the 150 years since Mendel proposed his laws of genetics. We now know that the relationship between gene and trait can be much more complicated than those seen in the orderly behavior of pea plants. But Mendel's basic laws of inheritance have been confirmed countless times, and so has the physical existence of genes, the invisible units Mendel called heredity factors.

## The Discovery of the Chromosome

Where were these genes? And how exactly did parents pass them on to their children? The answers came slowly from the work of many different researchers. In 1882, a German scientist named Walther Fleming (1843–1905) published a book titled *Cell Substance, Nucleus, and Cell Division*. In it he described his work using dyes to study cells. He noticed that there was one structure inside cells that strongly absorbed dye, and he named it chromatin. He observed that right before cells divided, the chromatin separated into stringy objects. Later, other scientists would call these stringy objects chromosomes.

To describe the separation of the chromosomes, Fleming coined the term "mitosis." He did not realize, however, that

In 1900, the Dutch botanist Hugo de Vries *(above)* rediscovered Mendel's laws of genetics after reaching similar conclusions through his own independent research. The following year, Mendel's paper was translated into English for the first time.

what he observed had anything to do with inheritance. This was because Fleming, like most other scientists of his time, was unaware of Mendel's work, which had taken place about fifteen years earlier. Fleming wasn't looking for genes, so he didn't notice the connection.

In 1900, about two decades after Fleming published the results of his work, Dutch scientist Hugo de Vries (1848–1935) *was* looking for genes. Originally unaware of Mendel, de Vries independently concluded the existence of the gene and only later came across Gregor Mendel's historic paper. Around the same time, he discovered Walther Fleming's work, too. Putting together the evidence, he realized that the chromosomes Fleming had observed were probably genetic material. Mitosis was what happened after the chromosomes had been duplicated. Two identical copies of the complete set of chromosomes moved to opposite sides of the cell, which then split and became two identical cells with the same genetic material. The fact that the chromosomes were arranged in pairs during mitosis was very suggestive. Mendel thought that the genes came in twos (one from each parent), and here the chromosomes were coming in twos.

There was a puzzle associated with mitosis, though. After mitosis, each new cell had the same number of chromosomes contained in the one original cell before it split. Scientists observed this again and again under the microscope. This did not fit with Mendel's laws, which stated that a new generation of the children gets half its genetic material from each parent. It did not fit with common sense either. If both parents gave all their chromosomes to their children, each successive generation would have twice as many chromosomes as the previous generation. In fact, it is normal for individual organisms in a species to have exactly the same number of chromosomes. In human beings, the number is forty-six.

## Mitosis and Meiosis

The first person to propose a solution to this puzzle was German biologist August Weismann (1834–1914). In an 1892 book entitled *The Germ Plasm*, Weismann said that there were two types of cell division. One, mitosis, produced identical cells. This is what happens when our bodies grow. A skin cell or a muscle cell makes another one just like it, a clone with exact genetic inheritance. Another special kind of cell division occurs when bodies produce reproductive cells. (In human beings, the male sperm and the female egg, or ovum, are reproductive cells.) In that

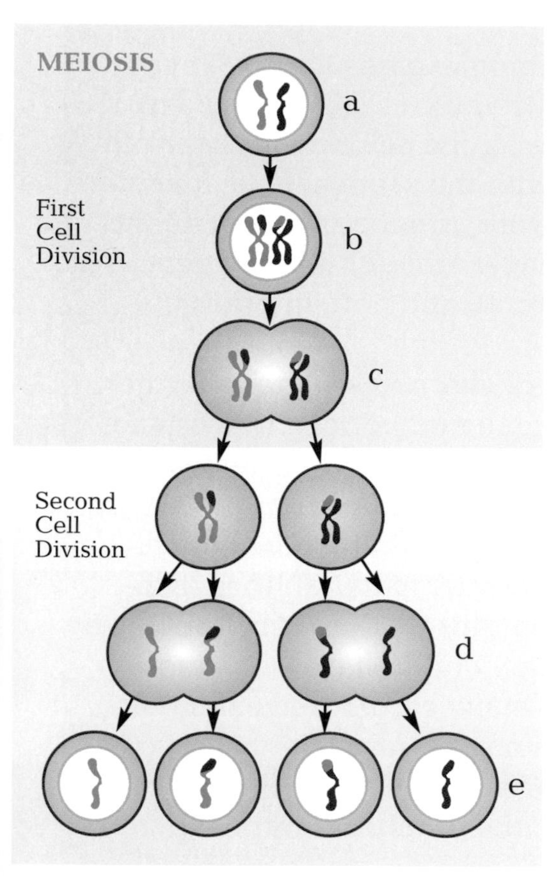


The first meiotic division begins with a single cell containing forty-six chromosomes (a). The chromosomes' DNA is replicated, or copied, and is recombined (b). The cell then divides into two cells (c). Because of recombination, each of these cells has a genetic makeup different from the original cell.

In the second meiotic division, the cells split again (d). This time, however, the DNA is not replicated first. The result is four reproductive cells (e), each with twenty-three chromosomes.

case, the paired chromosomes separate, and the reproductive cell gets only one half of the pair.

Later research proved that Weismann was correct. Reproductive cells have half the number of chromosomes found in regular body cells. In human beings the number of chromosomes in a reproductive cell is twenty-three, half of forty-six. When our sex organs make reproductive cells, the chromosomes are copied. But the new copy then splits in half. The chromosomes, which are ordinarily paired, undergo disjunction, or separation. In disjunction, half of the chromosomes go to one reproductive cell and half go to another. The entire process that results in reproductive

## DOWN SYNDROME AND A MOTHER'S AGE

The odds of having a baby with Down syndrome increase with the mother's age. For women under age twenty-five, the odds of having a baby with Down syndrome are about 1 in 1,500. By age thirty-five, the risk increases to somewhere between 1 in 300 and 1 in 400. By age forty, the odds may be as high as 1 in 100 to 1 in 50, and by the mid-forties, the rate can be as high as 1 in 25.

We do not know the exact reason why children born to older mothers are more likely to have Down syndrome. It probably has to do with the age of the ova (egg cells) produced by the mother. Human females produce their egg cells before they are born. An ovum (a single egg cell) in a forty-five-year-old woman is forty-five years old. An error such as nondisjunction is more likely to occur in an egg that has been stored in an ovary for forty-five years. However, even though an older woman has a much greater chance of having a baby with Down syndrome, most children with Down syndrome—75 to 80 percent of them—are born to young women. This is simply because there are more young women than older women having babies.

cells with half the number of chromosomes as body cells is called meiosis.

Meiosis fit well with the laws of genetics. Mendel and other genetic researchers had shown that there were two genes per trait and that each parent contributed one and only one gene per trait. The splitting of the chromosomes during meiosis explained how that happened.

## Discovering the Structure of DNA

By the 1940s, scientists knew each chromosome was made of a single long strand of a molecule they called deoxyribonucleic acid (DNA). In the early 1950s, two young scientists, James D. Watson (1928–) and Francis Crick (1916–2004), achieved the greatest breakthrough in genetics since Mendel's original discoveries. Working together in Cambridge, England, these two men figured out the structure of the DNA molecule. In so doing, they also discovered what genes are made of and how they are copied. Their work led directly to our understanding of how DNA influences the way living things grow and behave.

Watson and Crick arrived at their model of DNA by using the known rules of chemical bonding. These rules state which atoms can form chemical bonds with which other atoms. Chemical analysis had shown which atoms were in a DNA molecule and in what proportions. Bonding rules limited the ways the DNA molecule could be put together. Using this information, Watson and Crick constructed a model. (They literally used a set of Tinkertoy-like pieces representing different atoms and groups of atoms.) In the end, they had a three-dimensional model of a section of DNA. When Watson and Crick had assembled a model that fit the bonding rules and included all the pieces, they found that it also explained how DNA works.

## Four Nucleotides

Watson and Crick's model describes DNA as a double-helix, a structure that resembles a spiral staircase. The steps of the staircase are pairs of chemical units called nucleotides. Each

James Watson *(left)* and Francis Crick *(right)* are shown with their model of DNA. In 1953, Watson and Crick used the model to deduce the structure of DNA, the molecule that makes up genes. For their pioneering work, the two men received the 1962 Nobel Prize for Physiology or Medicine.

nucleotide is made up of a deoxyribose sugar molecule plus one of four bases—adenine, thymine, cytosine, or guanine. For simplicity, scientists refer to these nucleotides as A (adenine), T (thymine), C (cytosine), and G (guanine). These nucleotides can appear in any order in the DNA molecule.

Watson and Crick's model shows not only how DNA looks, it also shows how DNA works as a carrier of biological inheritance. It shows, first of all, how DNA is copied. Each kind of nucleotide bonds with only one other kind of nucleotide. The adenine-containing nucleotide pairs with

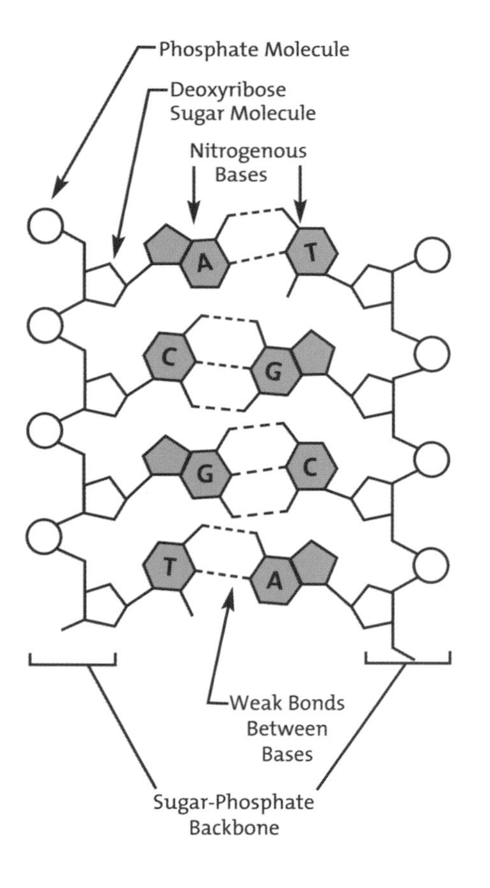


This two-dimensional diagram shows the chemical structure of a DNA molecule. The phosphate and sugar molecules form the two "backbones" of the double-helix structure. The actual DNA molecule is also surrounded by a protein envelope, which protects it. During cell division, the molecule splits along the weak bonds between bases.

only the thymine-containing nucleotide, and the guanine-containing nucleotide fits with only the cytosine-containing nucleotide. So, A pairs only with T, and vice versa; C pairs only with G, and vice versa.

The model shows how, during both mitosis and meiosis, the DNA molecule "unzips." In other words, it splits lengthwise, leaving two halves of the DNA staircase made of the two opposite series of base pairs. Assisted by other molecules, each half of the DNA molecule becomes complete again. This series of transformations results in the production of two complete DNA molecules—two copies of the original.

Francis Crick also played an important role in the discovery of how DNA carries information. In his later work, Crick suggested that DNA was a code, a set of instructions written in the four nucleotides, A, T, C, and G. The chemical bases that formed the steps of the DNA staircase were like letters that spelled out sentences. The makeup of "sentences" determined the functions of the genes that contained them.

Finally, further research in the 1950s and 1960s explained what these "sentences" (the genes) actually do to determine biological traits. Each gene, with the help of other molecules in the cell, produces a protein. Genes, in other words, are instructions, and based on these instructions, the body makes proteins. There are many kinds of proteins, and they do many different jobs in the body. Some are like building blocks, helping to form tissues like bone and muscle. Others are enzymes, organic molecules that speed up chemical reactions. The many proteins that the genes code for are amazingly versatile and perform countless tasks within our bodies.

## An Extra Chromosome

As research since Gregor Mendel's day has shown, the process by which genes are handed down from parents to children is incredibly complex. That it occurs at all is a miracle. But there is bound to be an error now and then in any process that involves so many steps. Errors that sometimes occur during cell reproduction are what cause genetic diseases and disorders.

What is the error behind Down syndrome? In 1932, Petrus Johannes Waardenburg suggested that the culprit in Down syndrome might be a problem during meiosis, the process that creates reproductive cells. You already read that one step of meiosis involves disjunction—the moment when the pairs of chromosomes separate. Scientists had noticed that sometimes disjunction didn't happen correctly. A pair of chromosomes, for some reason, could remain stuck to each other. Whenever this occurred, one reproductive cell did not get a copy of a particular chromosome, and another reproductive cell got two copies. The result would be a child who had either one less or one more chromosome than the usual number.

In the 1930s, it was practically impossible to test Waardenburg's hypothesis because individual human chromosomes are difficult to see, even under a microscope. Biologists were not even sure how many chromosomes were in a complete set. In the early 1950s, however, scientists developed new chemical solutions that made chromosomes condense and separate so that they were easier to count. In 1959, two scientists working separately—Jérôme Lejeune (1926–1994) in France, and Patricia Jacobs (1934–) in England—confirmed Waardenburg's theory about the probable cause of Down syndrome.

## Trisomy 21

People normally have forty-six chromosomes, but people with Down syndrome have forty-seven chromosomes. They have received an extra chromosome from one of their parents, usually the mother. The chromosome pair affected is always the same one, the one scientists label number 21. Ninety-five percent of all cases of Down syndrome are caused by this condition, which physicians and scientists call trisomy 21, meaning three copies of chromosome 21. Instead of having two almost identical versions of chromosome 21, people with Down syndrome have three. In most cases, the extra chromosome, along with all the others, is present in every cell of the body of a person with Down syndrome.

Why should an extra chromosome cause such effects? The answer lies in the complex ways that genes influence

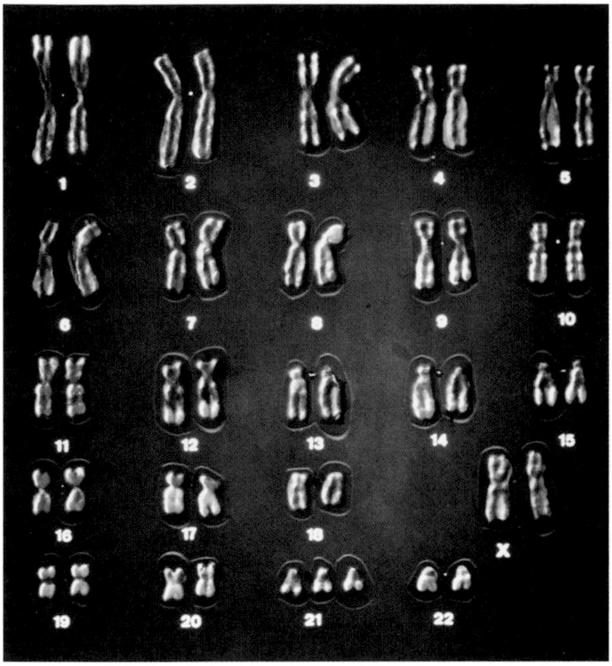

A karyotype is a photograph used to check for chromosomal abnormalities. To create a karyotype, scientists stain a cell's chromosomes with dye and photograph them through a microscope. The photograph is then cut up, and the chromosomes are numbered and arranged in pairs. This karyotype shows three copies of chromosome 21, indicating Down syndrome.

human traits. As you have learned, genes tell the body to produce proteins. Many genes create proteins that regulate other genes. The amount of protein produced can matter a great deal. Having an extra gene may mean that an extra amount of the protein will be produced. Too much of a given protein may upset the function of other proteins. In other cases, many different proteins combine to form large, complex structures in the cell. When that happens, the amount of the protein produced can make a difference in the cell's structure.

Scientists still do not know what causes nondisjunction. Nor do they know exactly which of the hundreds of genes on chromosome 21 are involved in expressing the characteristics of Down syndrome. Nevertheless, trisomy 21 explains the similarities among people with Down syndrome. It explains why unrelated people with the disorder have slanting eyes; a low, short nose; intellectual disabilities; a certain way of walking; short stature; and (often) a malformation of the heart. These traits are all related to genes on chromosome 21.

## Translocation

About 3 to 4 percent of all cases of Down syndrome result from another chromosome defect called translocation. In this case, chromosome 21 attaches to another chromosome, forming a single chromosome. When the other chromosome involved is chromosome 14, the new combined chromosome is called t(14,21). (The other chromosomes that are sometimes involved are chromosomes 13, 15, and 22.) In this case, as a result of translocation, all the cells of the body have two copies of chromosome 21, one of chromosome 14, and one of t(14,21). Since, in effect, there is a complete extra set of chromosome 21 genes, the result is Down syndrome.

Scientists do not know why translocation happens. Like nondisjunction, it just seems to be one of many possible errors that can occur in the delicate, multistep process of genetic copying. Translocation can affect any chromosome, but embryos that have translocation of chromosomes other than chromosome 21 do not survive long. They become early miscarriages.

Translocation is inheritable, so people who do not have outward signs of Down syndrome can still be carriers of the condition. Unaffected carriers have one copy each of chromosomes 21, 14, and t(14,21), but they have no extra chromosome 21, so they do not have Down syndrome. Unaffected carriers of t(14,21) are said to be "balanced" because they have the right number of each chromosome. If a mother (and only the mother) is a balanced carrier of t(14,21), there is about a 12 percent chance that her child will have Down syndrome. If the father (and only the father) is a balanced carrier, the chance that he will produce a child with Down syndrome is about 3 percent.

## Mosaicism

In addition to those who have Down syndrome because of trisomy 21 and translocation, about 1 to 2 percent of people with the disorder have a different and sometimes less severe version called mosaic Down syndrome. In mosaic Down syndrome, some cells of the body have trisomy 21—the extra chromosome 21—and some are normal. The genetic difference among the body's trillions of cells, like the differences in color among the pieces of a mosaic, suggested the name. Mosaicism can occur in two different, though related, ways.

In the first case, the trisomy 21 defect occurs when a fertilized egg begins to divide to become an embryo. The embryo is composed of identical cells called stem cells. These will later divide and become the specialized cells for all of the different parts of the body. In the course of the early series of cell divisions, disjunction fails, and one or more of the stem cells is affected. Only the body cells descended from these stem cells have the extra chromosome 21.

In the second case, the original fertilized egg has trisomy 21, but the disjunction error is naturally corrected in some of the stem cells. The result, again, is mosaicism. Some cells in the embryo have three copies of chromosome 21, and some cells have the usual two copies.

As a group, children with mosaicism have less severe cases of Down syndrome, scoring slightly higher on IQ tests.

# Living with Down Syndrome

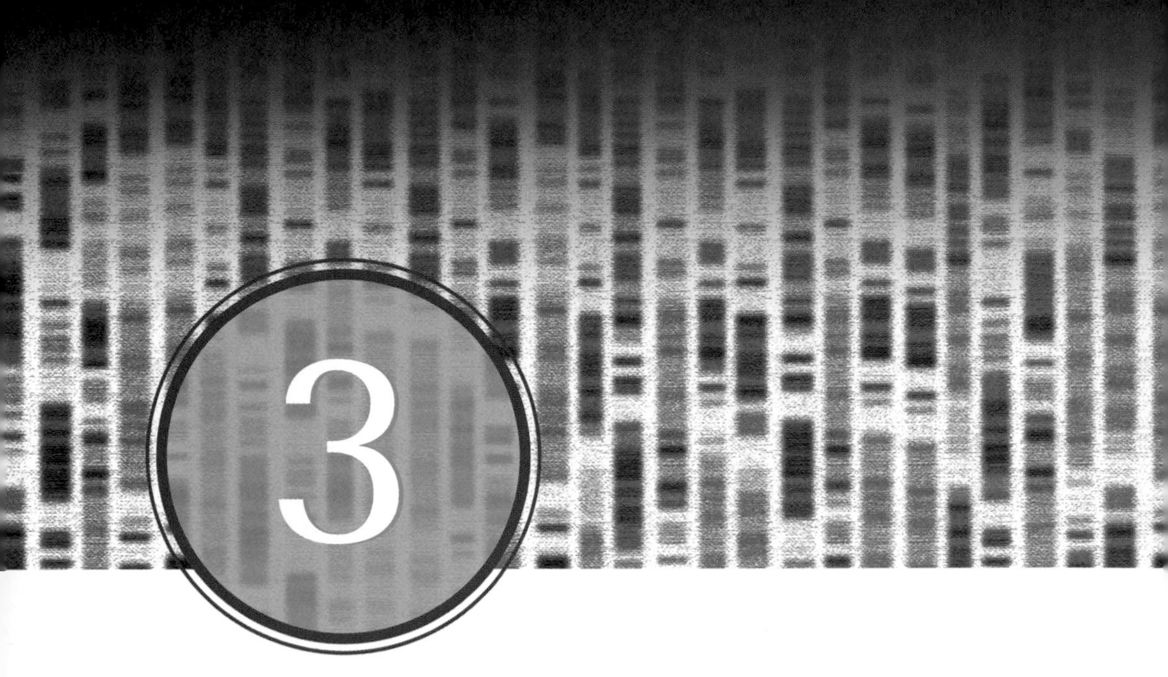


Over the years, better care, better education, and medical advances have dramatically improved the mental functioning and general health of people with Down syndrome. The life expectancy of a person with the disorder is about double what it was thirty years ago. According to the U.S. Centers for Disease Control and Prevention (CDC), the average age at death rose to forty-nine in 1997, up from twenty-five in 1983.

The future holds promise for even more fundamental improvements in the lives of people with Down syndrome. So far, though, the most important changes that have occurred are the result of major shifts in public attitudes. These shifts are part of a

A fifty-seven-year-old man with Down syndrome hugs his mother, who has cared for her son all his life. Life expectancy for those with Down syndrome has steadily increased in the past few decades. Reaching age fifty-seven, however, is exceptional.

general revolution in the approach to individuals with disabilities in our society.

## Changing the Old Attitudes

In the 1940s and 1950s, millions of mothers and mothers-to-be looked to the best-selling book *Baby and Child Care* for guidance on child rearing. Written by Dr. Benjamin Spock (1903–1998), the book advised that babies born with Down syndrome should immediately be institutionalized. That is, they should be sent to live in a hospital-like facility where professionals would care for them. "If the infant exists at a level that is hardly human," Spock wrote, "it is much better for the other children and parents to have him cared for elsewhere."

Spock's advice wasn't the result of any special heartlessness in him. It was what most doctors believed at the time.

We now know, however, that Spock and his fellow pediatricians were wrong. Later advancement in the treatment of children with Down syndrome proved that they are quite sociable and suffer psychologically when they are institutionalized. The mid-twentieth-century approach to Down syndrome—separating the children from their families, and separating them from other children—was as mistaken as John Langdon Down's theory that his patients were throwbacks to some prehistoric common ancestor of Europeans and Asians. The results of this attitude were tragic for the children with Down syndrome, who generally received care that was inferior to the care they would have received at home. It was also difficult for the parents, who had to live with the guilt of abandoning a child.

## Children with Down Syndrome

Like other children, children with Down syndrome are happiest and healthiest living in a loving home. Like other children, they also need stimulation and a variety of social contacts. Research shows that children with Down syndrome growing up in families progress faster and achieve more than children with the disorder growing up in institutions. Professionals, no matter how well trained, are not better than family members at caring for children. Research also shows that children with Down syndrome who are mainstreamed (put in regular classes with children without disabilities) progress at a faster rate and achieve more than children with Down syndrome who learn in special-education settings.

Studies and surveys also have something to say about the experience of the families of children with Down syndrome. Raising a child with Down syndrome is a profound challenge, bringing special worries about the child's health, education,

This six-year-old boy with Down syndrome is learning in a main-stream classroom—one in which the other students do not have disabilities. According to the National Down Syndrome Congress, most people with Down syndrome graduate from high school. Some later enroll in colleges and vocational programs.

and his or her future. But these worries generally do not destroy families or weaken them.

This is not to deny that it is difficult to raise a child with a lifelong health problem or disability. Children and adults with Down syndrome often have an impaired immune system and may frequently become ill. Despite improvements in medical treatment, many people with Down syndrome die in childhood or in early youth, usually because of heart defects. Raising a child who is ill and who may die young can be a terrible ordeal for families, but many parents have met the challenge with a positive attitude.

**PEOPLE WITH DOWN SYNDROME SPEAKING FOR THEMSELVES**

"My name is Gabrielle Clark. I am nearly nineteen and I have Down syndrome, I don't suffer from it as many people say, I just have it. I was born that way. My mother told me when I was very little that I had Down syndrome (Probably the day I was born, she's like that you know, always explaining the truth). I still don't understand completely what it means except that I have an extra chromosome and that I look a bit different and, Oh yeah, I'm supposed to be a bit slow. (My mum says I've never been slow in my life, but she's my mum and she's prejudiced.)"

—Quoted in Sue Buckley's *Living with Down Syndrome*

## Parents' Perspective

In a study conducted in the late 1980s, all sixteen parents surveyed reported that raising a child with Down syndrome had a profound impact on their lives. All reported that the positive aspects outweighed the negative. Parents in this study said that having a child with Down syndrome had brought the family closer together, taught them the meaning of unconditional love, "put things in perspective," and taught them the importance of diversity. As one parent interviewed for the study put it, as quoted in *Genetic Disease*, "At the time [of the diagnosis], you feel that this is the biggest tragedy that ever happened. If we could have known what it would be like to have M., we wouldn't have been nearly so sad. No one really mentioned the positive side." In a 1996 paper about long-term studies of families with Down syndrome, writer C. C. Cunningham concluded the following:

> The overriding impression of the families and their child with Down syndrome is one of normality. The factors that influence the well being of all members are largely the same as those influencing any child or family. The majority of families did not exhibit pathology as a consequence of having a child with Down syndrome. [That is, the families were normal.] Indeed the evidence points to positive effects for many families when one member has Down syndrome.

## Different Needs

Children and adults with Down syndrome are not all alike. They have different needs, different personalities, and different potential for achievement in life. Some are self-confident and outgoing and have active social lives. Some are drawn to sports, engaging and excelling in swimming, gymnastics, water skiing, or riding. Others are placid and shy, preferring quiet activities with a few friends.

Babies with Down syndrome grow and develop like other babies, but at a slower pace. They tend to reach developmental milestones later than other children. For instance, a child who develops normally usually learns to walk at twelve to fourteen months. A child with Down syndrome, on the other hand, might learn to walk between eighteen and thirty-six months. Similarly, first words and sentences will come later than with other children.

Some people with Down syndrome have intellectual abilities that are within the normal range; the majority have a

Children with Down syndrome typically have weakened immune systems, so parents need to monitor their health closely. According to data from the National Institutes of Health, children with Down syndrome are more susceptible than others to ear and throat infections. In addition, they are much more likely to develop infectious respiratory illnesses like pneumonia.

moderate degree of intellectual disability. The lifestyles that people with Down syndrome lead depend on innate physical differences and differences of ability. But they also depend, to a great degree, on the support they get from both professionals and family. Children with Down syndrome often attend regular schools in regular classes, with differing levels of support. Most young people with Down syndrome graduate from high school. Some are enrolled in postsecondary educational programs, including colleges and vocational programs. Like the rest of us, people with Down syndrome continue to learn and progress throughout their lives.

Many adults with Down syndrome have jobs. Some work in special settings designed for people with disabilities. Others hold jobs they find themselves on the open labor market. Adults with Down syndrome live in a variety of settings—by themselves or with roommates in apartments, condominiums, or houses; in special facilities called group homes that have support services; or with family members.

## Sex and Down Syndrome

Sex is a complicated matter for everyone. It can be even more complicated for those of us who have physical or intellectual disabilities. For many years, society as a whole preferred to treat people with Down syndrome as if they were children, both physically and emotionally. But the fact is that as people with Down syndrome approach adolescence, their bodies undergo the normal physical and hormonal changes of puberty. They have the same emotions, desires, and confusions that all people experience. So, naturally, they become interested in dating, marriage, and parenthood. Along with these concerns, they also have to cope with the possibility of unwanted pregnancy, sexually transmitted diseases, and fending off unwanted sexual advances. Medical and psychological experts tend to agree that it is usually best to educate people with Down syndrome about sexual matters. With the proper individualized instruction and education, people with Down syndrome can develop appropriate sexual behavior and make informed choices for themselves.

It is not uncommon for people with Down syndrome to marry. Often, their spouses have Down syndrome, too. In these cases, couples are usually supported closely and consistently by health care professionals and family members alike.

If these couples decide to have children, they go through counseling, just like many prospective parents.

Based on the available statistics, the National Down Syndrome Society reports that about 50 percent of women with the disorder are fertile, or able to have children. Approximately half of the children born to mothers with Down syndrome also have the disorder or some other developmental disability.

For a long time, researchers thought men with Down syndrome were infertile. However, recent studies indicate that men with the disorder can, in fact, father children. The data is insufficient to determine whether the children of men with Down syndrome have increased likelihood of inheriting the disorder.

## Other Complications

The health problems of children and adults with Down syndrome vary greatly. About one-third to one-half of the people with the disorder suffer from heart defects. Heart malformations include abnormal openings in the walls that separate the heart's chambers, a condition that can cause abnormal blood flow within the heart. These problems require very close attention. They are treated with medications and frequently with surgery.

A small minority of people with Down syndrome have other mental disorders such as autism, a brain disorder that impairs a person's ability to communicate and to understand emotions. People with Down syndrome are also more prone to develop Alzheimer's disease, a degenerative brain condition that impairs mental functioning in the elderly. For the general population, people who develop Alzheimer's disease usually begin to show symptoms between fifty and seventy-five years of age. But for people with Down syndrome who develop the disease, the average age of onset is between thirty and thirty-five years old.

# Testing for Down Syndrome

4

As you have learned already, advances in medical science have improved the physical and mental health of people with Down syndrome. Medical science is also the key to testing whether unborn children have Down syndrome.

Several tests are used to determine the probability that a mother is carrying a fetus with Down syndrome. Some of the tests are without risk to the baby, so they are performed in most pregnancies. Other tests can cause the mother to miscarry, so they are done only if the results of earlier tests indicate a high risk of a genetic defect.

The tests are not perfect. The low-risk tests are not very accurate, and even the riskier tests are not 100 percent accurate. They sometimes fail to detect a case of Down syndrome,

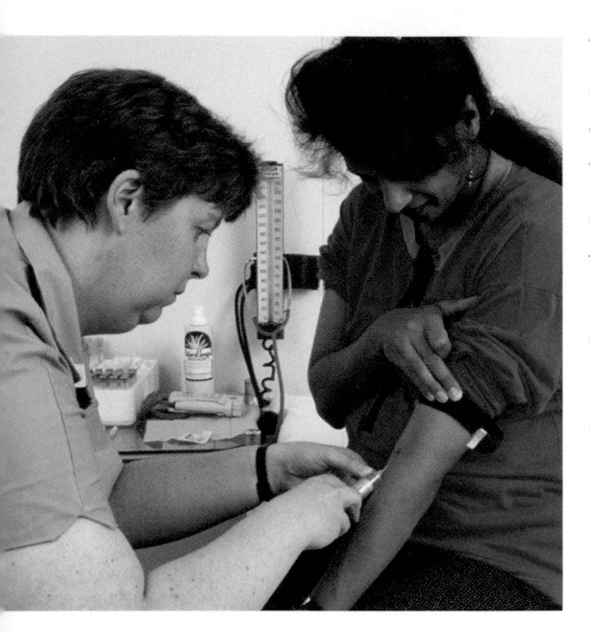

This midwife is taking a blood sample from a pregnant woman. The expectant mother's blood can be tested for a variety of disorders. Depending on their purpose, the blood tests are known by different names, including maternal serum screening test, multiple marker screening test, triple screen, and quad screen, among others.

and sometimes they yield a false positive, indicating that a fetus has Down syndrome when in fact it does not. For these reasons, most prenatal (before birth) testing for Down syndrome is done for women who are over thirty-five years old and therefore at increased risk of having a baby with trisomy 21.

There are usually forty weeks between the conception and the birth of a baby. Today doctors know a great deal about the changes that go on in a woman's body during this period. This knowledge provides the basis for prenatal detection of genetic disorders.

## Blood Tests

In general, blood tests for Down syndrome are performed between the fourteenth and sixteenth week of pregnancy. These tests, performed on a blood sample taken from the mother, check the levels of certain proteins and hormones

## NEW DEVELOPMENTS IN PRENATAL DOWN SYNDROME SCREENING

Researchers recently published the results of an eight-year study of prenatal screening for Down syndrome. The study, which cost $15 million and involved more than 38,000 women, indicates that screening tests produce more accurate results when done earlier. For instance, when blood and ultrasound tests were performed during the eleventh week of pregnancy, the results were accurate in 87 percent of the cases. With tests done during the usual sixteenth week of pregnancy, the figure was closer to 81 percent. Not only are the earlier tests more accurate, but mothers-to-be can also ease their minds earlier. Based on the results of this study, physicians may eventually recommend that some at-risk women undergo screening at an earlier date.

(chemical messengers). The proteins and hormones are present in greater quantities when the fetus has Down syndrome. About 60 to 80 percent of fetuses with Down syndrome can be detected by considering the results of these blood tests together with the mother's age.

## Ultrasound

An ultrasound examination is another test performed in almost all pregnancies in developed countries today. It is a low-risk procedure than can tell physicians a lot about the fetus. Ultrasound uses high-frequency sound waves to create images of the inside of the body. Unlike an X-ray, however,

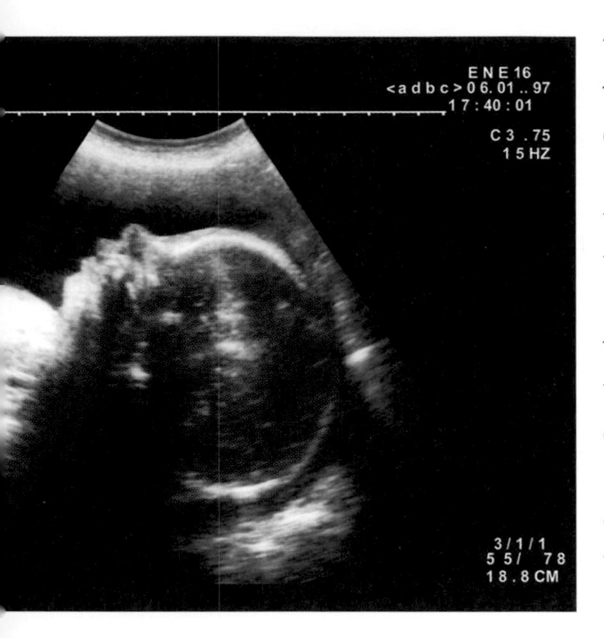


This ultrasound image shows the head of a fetus during the eighth month of pregnancy. Ultrasound imaging can help physicians determine if a fetus is at an increased risk of having Down syndrome. It is important to note, however, that ultrasound helps predict but cannot be used to diagnose. For a true diagnosis of the disorder, the fetus's chromosomes must be examined.

the ultrasound can show moving images in real time. During ultrasound exams, a technician puts gel on the outside of the mother's belly and moves a sensor across her skin. A computer program translates the ultrasound information into an image on a TV monitor. During ultrasound exams, physicians look for physical indications of Down syndrome. These include a thickening of the skin at the back of the neck, bright spots on the kidneys or heart, short arms or legs, or reduced head size. If any of these physical markers are observed, other testing is generally recommended.

## Amniocentesis

If the risk of Down syndrome—or any other genetic disorder—is considered high, a procedure called amniocentesis may be performed, usually around the sixteenth week of pregnancy. Amniocentesis involves testing amniotic fluid, the liquid in which the fetus is suspended. First, an ultrasound examination is done to show the location of the amniotic cavity and the fetus. Then, a needle is inserted into the amniotic cavity through the mother's abdomen, and a small amount of amniotic fluid is drawn up through the needle. The amniotic fluid contains cells from the fetus. These cells are cultured—that is, grown—and then they are tested for chromosomal abnormalities. It usually takes between twelve and twenty days to obtain the results.

Amniocentesis is a relatively accurate predictor of Down syndrome, but it is a risky procedure. It can lead to infection, bleeding, or cramping. The needle can also accidentally puncture the skin of the fetus. Amniocentesis causes miscarriage about 1 out of every 500 times it is performed.

## Chorionic Villus Sampling

Another test for chromosomal abnormalities, including Down syndrome, is chorionic villus sampling (CVS). CVS is done early in pregnancy, usually between nine and twelve weeks after conception. As in the amniocentesis procedure, ultrasound is done first. Then a thin tube is inserted through the vagina or abdomen, and a small piece of the placenta is removed. The placenta is a temporary organ that connects the fetus to the mother, and its cells have the same chromosomes as the cells of the fetus. It takes about ten days to culture and examine the cells for chromosomal abnormalities. Studies show that when CVS is performed before the tenth week of pregnancy, there is an increased risk that the baby will be born with limb abnormalities that would not have occurred if the procedure had not been performed. In addition, the risk of miscarriage is slightly higher following CVS than with amniocentesis.

# Genetic Research and the Future of Down Syndrome

5

Research on basic therapies for Down syndrome is being conducted at many different kinds of institutions in the United States. For example, Stanford University School of Medicine has a Down Syndrome Research Center. In addition, private foundations, including the National Down Syndrome Society and the International Foundation for Genetics Research, award grants for promising research projects in Down syndrome. The U.S. government also funds Down syndrome research through the National Institutes of Health (NIH).

People with Down syndrome have an extra copy of chromosome 21, so the research that holds the most promise for helping them reveals the functions of the genes on chromosome 21.

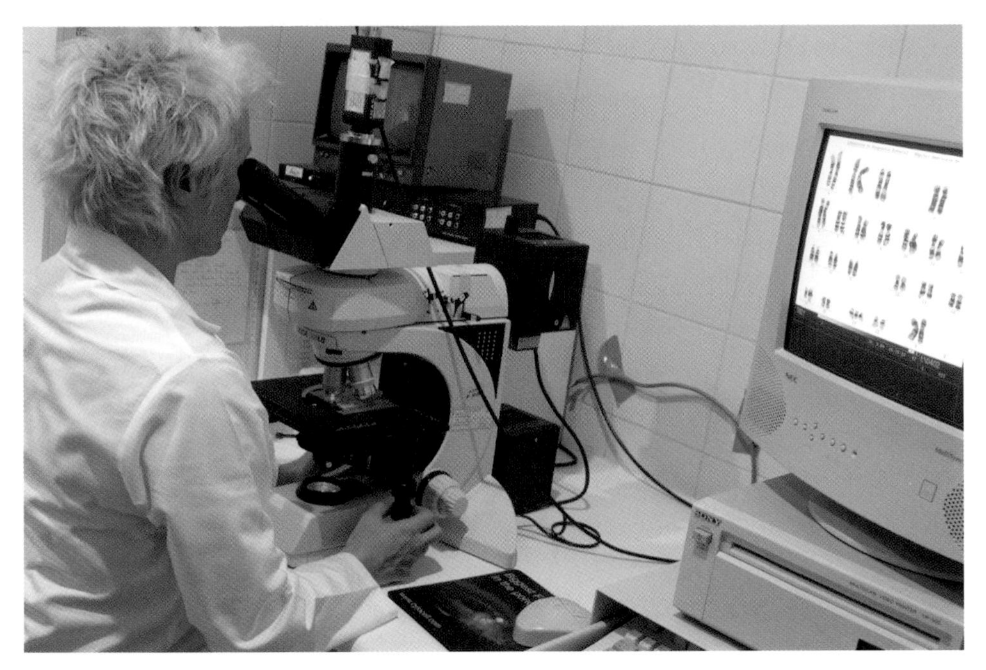

A researcher analyzes amniotic fluid, the liquid from the womb of a pregnant woman, which contains fetal cells. She is looking for evidence of trisomy 21, an indicator of Down syndrome. The fluorescence microscope she is using combines advanced optical components with computer technology.

This work tells researchers what happens when the genes work properly and what happens when there is an extra copy of the gene.

Understanding chromosome 21 is a great challenge. It contains 33.8 million nucleotide base pairs of DNA. Scientists currently estimate that these 33.8 million DNA base pairs probably contain the code for fewer than 300 genes. These are the genes that need to be precisely located on the chromosome to know which ones are involved in Down syndrome and how they interact.

## Stemming Protein Overproduction

The job of certain genes is to instruct the body to make a particular protein. An extra copy of a gene leads the body to make too much of that protein. Getting instructions from three genes instead of two, the body with Down syndrome produces more of a given protein, perhaps as much as 50 percent more. The results are very complicated because proteins do so many things in the human body and there are so many types of proteins.

Enzymes, for example, are proteins that make chemical reactions happen. Structural proteins are the building blocks of our body; they make up our hearts, lungs, bones, and skin. Hormones are proteins that act as chemical messengers, carrying signals between our cells. Receptor proteins make our senses work. The proteins actin and myosin make our heart and skeletal muscles move. The immune system helps the body fight off infection with proteins. Even DNA itself, which encodes the orders to produce proteins, is regulated by proteins called DNA-binding proteins.

All these proteins interact with each other in a complex way. So the overproduction of even one of them has unpredictable results. Eventually, we hope to know which proteins are overproduced. Then, we may be able to develop therapies that work by controlling—in most cases lowering—the function or production of chromosome 21 gene products that are involved in Down syndrome. One day, by identifying all the functions of the genes on chromosome 21, researchers will learn how they are implicated in Down syndrome. Ultimately, researchers may be able to develop specific treatments that lead the body back to the path of normal development.

## TOOLS OF GENETIC ENGINEERING

In the years since the discovery of the genetic code, researchers have developed many techniques for manipulating the DNA molecule. This science of changing DNA, called genetic engineering, makes use of naturally occurring processes.

One of the tools used in the laboratory is a group of organic proteins called restriction enzymes, which can cut DNA into small pieces. Researchers use viruses to import these snippets of DNA into bacterial cells, which make many copies of them. The principles are the same as those that are at work when we catch a cold virus. The virus infects our cells, takes over their DNA, and causes them to manufacture many copies of the virus.

Other viruses can be used to transport these multiplied DNA sequences into our own body cells, where they permanently change the behavior of those cells. Genetic researchers are using these techniques to map the human genome and discover what each gene does. Eventually these techniques might be used to treat genetic disorders.

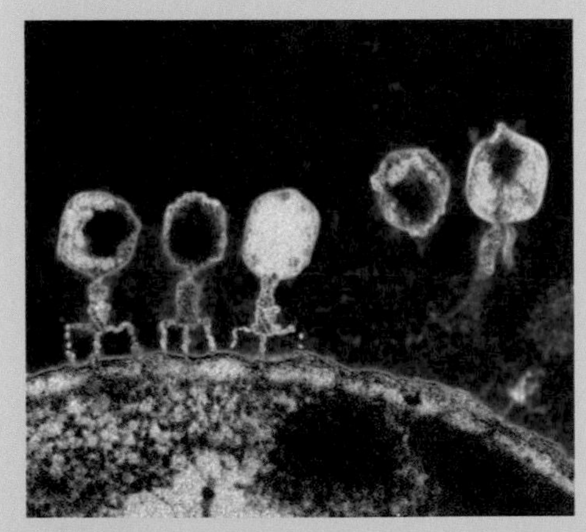

*This artificially colored image is called a transmission electron micrograph. It shows five blue viruses attacking a single brown bacterial cell. The three viruses already attached to the cell are injecting it with their genetic material, seen as blue strands. Scientists use viruses of this type, called bacteriophages, as a tool to modify genes.*

## Gene Therapy

Within the next few decades, physicians expect to be able to treat genetic diseases in people by directly changing the makeup of the DNA in the cells of patients' bodies. These new therapies will take advantage of a large assortment of biochemical tools that enable genetic researchers to manipulate DNA. (See sidebar on previous page.) These tools actually enable scientists to select small pieces of DNA from a chromosome, reproduce it many times, and reintroduce it into cells.

In the treatment of Down syndrome, gene therapy might one day be used to disable the genes on the extra copy of chromosome 21. With a normal complement of genes, the body cells of the Down syndrome patient would then behave normally. Many hurdles have to be overcome before this therapy can work, and there are some special problems that will make it difficult. For one thing, the gene therapy must disable one copy of chromosome 21 but not disrupt either of the other two. Otherwise the treatment would result in the death of cells. Another problem is that many of the problems of Down syndrome are the result of permanent damage that occurs early in life, mostly prior to birth. So gene therapy for Down syndrome might have to be administered to an unborn baby, an especially difficult medical and scientific challenge.

In addition, many people believe that gene therapy on humans presents an ethical problem. Some think that all genetic engineering is wrong. For these people, it is not up to humans to "correct" nature's errors. Others believe that some kinds of genetic engineering are acceptable but that a line must be drawn. Nobody argues that it is wrong to make life better for people with Down syndrome. However, many people fear that genetic engineering could lead to the creation of unpredictable organisms that could not occur naturally. As researchers continue to make technological advances, the debate is sure to continue.

## The Promise of Neurological Therapies

Using what is currently known about the way nerve cells transmit signals, drug companies have begun to develop medications that improve the way these cells function. The drugs that are currently used to slow down memory loss in patients with Alzheimer's disease are a product of this research. Alzheimer's disease is a degenerative brain disease that affects many people in old age. (In some people, however, it occurs in middle age.) Neurotransmitters are an especially important component of this research.

A class of natural chemicals, neurotransmitters control the nerve impulses in our brains. Many drugs in widespread use today lower or raise the levels of various neurotransmitters in the brain. Some researchers believe that existing drugs that affect neurotransmitter levels can help children with intellectual disabilities, including children with Down syndrome, to develop more normally. These researchers argue for intervention with drugs during a critical period in early childhood, when children's brains are rapidly developing.

Another kind of drug-based therapy for children with Down syndrome could make use of neurotrophins, chemicals that affect the way brains grow. Neurotrophins selectively encourage the growth of certain nerve cells in the brain. These nerve cells, or neurons, help us think. They also act as the communication system between sensory organs and the brain, as well as between the brain and muscles. So it is not surprising that abnormal nerve cell growth would affect the intelligence and reflexes. Studies of the brains of children with Down syndrome show that, overall, they have fewer nerve cells than is

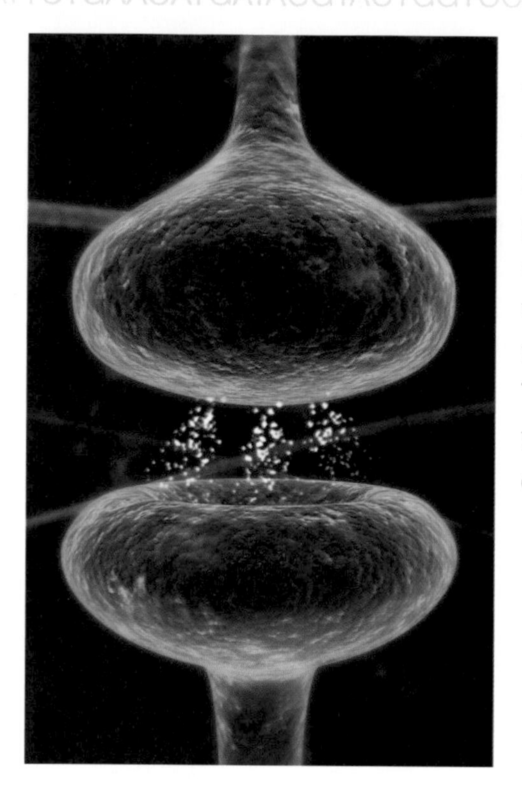

This is a computer-generated image of a synapse—the place at which nervous impulses pass from one neuron (nerve cell) to another. The small white particles in the gap represent neurotransmitters. These are chemicals that send nerve signals to structures called neuroreceptors.

normal. This may result from a failure to grow enough nerve cells, or it may be because the cells die off more rapidly than normal. Whatever the cause, one day, physicians may be able to use neurotrophins to raise the population of neurons in the brains of children with Down syndrome.

It is difficult to say how far away that day may be. It may take decades, because physicians and drug companies have to proceed slowly and methodically when they are developing new medicines for children. This is especially true with medicines for conditions—like Down syndrome—that are not an immediate threat to life.

Successful neurotrophin drug therapies have already been performed on mice that showed nerve degeneration due to aging. The first human beings who will use these drugs will probably be patients with Alzheimer's disease who are able to give informed consent to the use of an experimental drug.

Advanced medical and genetic therapies are the wave of the future in Down syndrome research. For the time being, however, traditional physical and speech therapy remain more important. Easter Seals is a nonprofit organization that offers such services for people with all kinds of disabilities, not just Down syndrome. These girls are having fun at an Easter Seals Walk With Me fundraiser.

When the safety of these drugs in adults is well established, physicians will be ready to try the drugs out to improve the lives of children with Down syndrome.

Other neurological therapies for children with Down syndrome may come as the result of research into other adult degenerative disorders that affect the brain, such as Huntington's disease and Parkinson's disease. In the meantime, the challenges of Down syndrome will continue to engage and inspire scientists and researchers. At the same time, the disorder will continue to confront all of us with our need to cherish the differences as well as the similarities among human beings.

# Timeline

**1866**
Gregor Mendel publishes his findings on the principles of heredity; John Langdon Down publishes the first thorough clinical description of individuals with Down syndrome.

**1900**
Hugo de Vries rediscovers Mendel's laws of genetics.

**1932**
Petrus Waardenburg guesses that Down syndrome may be the result of a chromosomal defect caused by nondisjunction, the failure of a pair of chromosomes to separate during meiosis.

**1944**
Oswald Theodore Avery (1877–1955) and his coworkers describe DNA (deoxyribonucleic acid) as the hereditary material.

**1946**
Benjamin Spock suggests in his best-selling parenting guide, *Baby and Child Care*, that babies born with Down syndrome should immediately be institutionalized.

**1953**
James D. Watson and Francis Crick describe the double-helix structure of DNA.

**1959**
Jérôme Lejeune, Marthe Gautier, and M. Raymond Turpin confirm the hypothesis that claims Down syndrome is caused by nondisjunction.

**1961**
The National Association for Down Syndrome, a Down syndrome advocacy and support group, is founded.

**1967**
C. B. Jacobson and R. H. Barter use amniocentesis for the first time in a prenatal diagnosis of a genetic disorder.

**1970**
Hamilton Smith, at Johns Hopkins University, discovers restriction enzymes. These are "molecular scissors" that protect bacteria by cutting the DNA in invading viruses.

**1975**
Edward Southern develops a method to isolate and analyze fragments of DNA.

**1979**
The National Down Syndrome Society, another advocacy and support group, is founded in New York City.

**1989**
Chris Burke stars as Corky Thatcher in ABC's hit television series *Life Goes On*, about a family with a teenager with Down syndrome.

**2000**
The chromosome 21 mapping and sequencing consortium publishes the gene sequence of chromosome 21 in the magazine *Nature*.

**2003**
In April, the International Human Genome Sequencing Consortium publishes the full sequence of the entire human genome.

# Glossary

**Alzheimer's disease** A degenerative disease of the central nervous system that leads to premature senile mental deterioration.

**amniocentesis** The surgical insertion of a hollow needle through the abdominal wall and into the uterus of a pregnant woman to obtain amniotic fluid, usually in order to detect a possible chromosomal abnormality in the fetus.

**amniotic fluid** The fluid in which an embryo is suspended.

**chorionic villus sampling (CVS)** A diagnostic procedure in which fetal cells are obtained from the placenta of a pregnant woman.

**chromosome** A structure containing most or all of an organism's genes; humans normally have forty-six chromosomes.

**deoxyribonucleic acid (DNA)** The molecules inside cells that carry genetic information and pass it from one generation to the next.

**embryo** An unborn animal in the early stages of growth.

**enzymes** Proteins produced by the body that greatly accelerate the rate of specific biochemical reactions.

**fetus** A developing human, usually from three months after conception to birth.

**gene** A length of DNA (a series of nucleotides) on a chromosome; the functional unit of inheritance.

**genetic disorder** A disease linked to the basic processes of biological inheritance.

**hormone** A product of living cells that circulates in the body and produces a specific effect on cells far from its point of origin.

**human genome** The full collection of genes needed to produce a human being.

**Huntington's disease** A hereditary degenerative nervous disorder marked by uncontrollable movements of the limbs and facial muscles.

**mainstream** To educate a student with a disability in a class with students without disabilities.

**mongolism** An early name for Down syndrome; it is no longer used to describe the condition and is generally considered offensive.

**mosaicism** A condition in which different cells of the body have different genetic makeups.

**neurological** Relating to the nervous system.

**neurons** Nerve cells.

**neurotrophins** Chemicals that selectively encourage the growth of nerve cells.

**nondisjunction** The failure of a pair of chromosomes to separate during cell division; the major cause of trisomy 21, which results in Down syndrome.

**ovum** A female sex cell, which contains half the genetic material the offspring will receive. The plural is "ova."

**Parkinson's disease** A progressive nervous disease that usually occurs late in life, marked by tremors and muscle weakness.

**pathology** Illness.

**prenatal** Prior to birth.

**restriction enzymes** Enzymes that break DNA into fragments at specific sites.

**translocation** A chromosomal abnormality in which a part of a chromosome is transferred to a nonhomologous (dissimilar) chromosome; sometimes a cause of Down syndrome.

**trisomy 21** The condition of having an extra chromosome 21; the principle cause of Down syndrome.

**ultrasound** A diagnostic procedure that uses high-frequency sound waves to produce two-dimensional or three-dimensional images for the assessment of internal body structures.

# For More Information

Down Syndrome Research Foundation
1409 Sperling Avenue
Burnaby, BC V5B 4J8
Canada
(604) 444-3773
Web site: http://dsrf.org

National Down Syndrome Congress
1370 Center Drive, Suite 102
Atlanta, GA 30338
(800) 232-6372
Web site: http://www.ndsccenter.org

National Down Syndrome Society
666 Broadway
New York, NY 10012
(800) 221-4602
Web site: http://www.ndss.org

National Human Genome Research Institute
National Institutes of Health
Communications and Public Liaison Branch
Building 31, Room 4B09

31 Center Drive, MSC 2152
9000 Rockville Pike
Bethesda, MD 20892-2152
(301) 402-0911
Web site: http://www.genome.gov

## Web Sites

Due to the changing nature of Internet links, the Rosen Publishing Group, Inc., has developed an online list of Web sites related to the subject of this book. This site is updated regularly. Please use this link to access the list:

http://www.rosenlinks.com/gdd/dosy

# For Further Reading

Boon, Kevin A. *The Human Genome Project: What Does Decoding DNA Mean for Us?* Berkeley Heights, NJ: Enslow, 2002.

Bowman-Kruhm, Mary. *Everything You Need to Know About Down Syndrome*. New York, NY: Rosen Publishing Group, 1999.

Hamilton, Janet. *James Watson: Solving the Mystery of DNA*. Berkeley Heights, NJ: Enslow, 2004.

Kafka, Tina. *DNA on Trial*. San Diego, CA: Lucent, 2004.

Klare, Roger. *Gregor Mendel: Father of Genetics*. Berkeley Heights, NJ: Enslow, 1997.

Krasnow, David. *Genetics*. Milwaukee, WI: Gareth Stevens Publishing, 2003.

Pueschel, Siegfried. *A Parent's Guide to Down's Syndrome: Toward a Brighter Future*. Rev. ed. Baltimore, MD: Brookes Publishing, 2000.

Snedden, Robert. *Cell Division and Genetics*. Portsmouth, NH: Heinemann, 2002.

Snedden, Robert. *DNA and Genetic Engineering*. Portsmouth, NH: Heinemann, 2002.

Tocci, Salvatore. *Down Syndrome*. New York, NY: Venture Books, 2000.

# Bibliography

Capone, George T. "Down Syndrome: Genetic Insights and Thoughts on Early Intervention." *Infants & Young Children*, Vol. 17, No. 1, January–March 2004, pp. 45–58.

Cohen, William I., Lynne Nadel, and Myra E. Madnick, eds. *Down Syndrome: Visions for the 21st Century*. New York, NY: Wiley-Liss, 2002.

Cunningham, C. "Families of Children with Down Syndrome." *Down Syndrome: Research and Practice*, Vol. 4, No. 3, 1996, pp. 87–95.

Dunn, L. C. *A Short History of Genetics: The Development of Some of the Main Lines of Thought: 1864–1939*. New York, NY: McGraw-Hill, 1965.

Hawley, R. Scott, and Catherine A. Mori. *The Human Genome: A User's Guide*. New York, NY: Academic Press, 1999.

Rainer, John D., ed. *Genetic Disease: The Unwanted Inheritance*. Binghamton, NY: Haworth Press, 1989.

Shapiro, Robert. *The Human Blueprint: The Race to Unlock the Secrets of Our Genetic Script*. New York, NY: St. Martin's Press, 1991.

Stray-Gunderson, Karen. *Babies with Down Syndrome: A New Parent's Guide*. Bethesda, MD: Woodbine House, 1995.

Van Riper, Marcia. "Living with Down Syndrome." *Down Syndrome Quarterly*, Vol. 4, No. 1, March 1999. Retrieved August 15, 2005 (http://www.denison.edu/collaborations/dsq/vanriper.html).

# Index

## About the Author

Phillip Margulies has written many books on health and medicine for young readers, including a series on epidemic diseases, their history, causes, and cures. Other titles by the author include *West Nile Virus*, *Diphtheria*, *Creutzfeldt-Jakob Disease*, and *Everything You Need to Know about Rheumatic Fever*. He lives in New York City with his wife, two children, and a high-spirited cocker spaniel named Jeptha.

## Photo Credits

Cover top, p. 27 © CNRI/Photo Researchers, Inc; cover inset, p. 1 © Lawrence Lawry/Photodisc/PunchStock; cover background images: © www.istockphoto.com/Rafal Zdeb (front right), © www.istockphoto.com/Arnold van Rooij (front middle), © Jim Wehtie/Photodisc/PunchStock (back right), © www.istockphoto.com (back middle, back left); p. 5 © Wellcome Photo Library; pp. 7, 8 © United States National Library of Medicine, National Institutes of Health; p. 10 © Hulton-Deutsch Collection/ Corbis; p. 13 © Biophoto Associates/Photo Researchers, Inc.; p. 16 © Hulton Archive/Getty Images; p. 18 © Bettmann/Corbis; p. 23 © A. Barrington Brown/Photo Researchers, Inc.; p. 24 U.S. Department of Energy Human Genome Program, http://www.ornl.gov/hgmis; p. 31 © Bill Snead/Lawrence Journal-World/AP/Wide World Photos; p. 33 © Lauren Shear/Photo Researchers, Inc.; p. 36 © Bruce Roberts/ Photo Researchers, Inc.; p. 40 © Jennie Woodcock/Reflections Photolibrary/Corbis; p. 42 © LADA/Photo Researchers, Inc.; p. 45 © Hop American/Photo Researchers, Inc.; p. 47 © Eye of Science/Science Photo Library; p. 50 © 3D4Medical.com/ Getty Images; p. 51 Chris Bond/Easter Seals of Missouri.

Designer: Evelyn Horovicz; Editor: Christopher Roberts
Photo Researcher: Hillary Arnold